For information address Disney • Lucasfilm Press,
1101 Flower Street, Glendale, California 91201.

Printed in China
First Hardcover Edition, July 2016   10 9 8 7 6 5 4 3 2 1

ISBN 978-1-4847-8700-7
FAC-023680-16195

Visit the official *Star Wars* website at: www.starwars.com
This book was printed on paper created from a sustainable source.

STAR WARS

The Battle of Yavin

Disney | LUCASFILM
PRESS

Los Angeles • New York

Book Four

Luke Skywalker still couldn't believe it. Just a few days before, he had been working on his uncle's moisture farm. Now he was worlds away from that desert planet, on Yavin's fourth moon. With the help of Han Solo and Chewbacca, he had delivered Princess Leia and the plans for the Death Star to the Rebel Alliance. Luke was going to help them destroy the Death Star. But the space station's weak spot would be very hard to hit. It was only two meters wide!

Luke reassured the other pilots: "I used to bull's-eye womp rats in my T-16 back home. They're not much bigger than two meters."

The rebels had to move fast. The Death Star was quickly making its way toward Yavin 4. One blast from the Death Star could destroy an entire planet in just seconds.

On board the Death Star, Darth Vader was feeling confident. He had already defeated Obi-Wan Kenobi, his old Jedi Master.

"This will be a day long remembered," Darth Vader told Death Star commander Grand Moff Tarkin. "It has seen the end of Kenobi. It will soon see the end of the Rebellion."

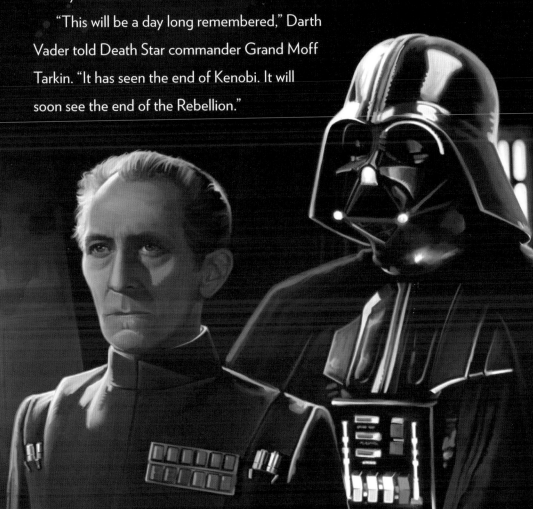

Meanwhile, back on Yavin, Luke quickly suited up in his pilot's uniform. As he made his way to his X-wing fighter, he saw Han Solo and Chewbacca loading up the *Millennium Falcon* to go. Chewie and Han had helped Luke and Leia escape the Death Star, but they weren't rebels—just smugglers who needed some fast money.

"Why don't you stay and fight with us?" Luke asked.

"What good's a reward if you ain't around to use it?" Han replied.

Luke walked away from Han and boarded his X-wing, shaking his head in disappointment.

On command, the fighters took off. Luke flew with Red Squadron, along with Wedge and his old friend Biggs from Tatooine. As he steered his X-wing toward the Death Star, he heard a voice—but it wasn't coming over the comm system. It was inside his head.

Luke, the Force will be with you.

The voice sounded like . . . Obi-Wan's? Luke wasn't sure, but he didn't have time to think. The Death Star came into view. It looked like a quiet metal moon, but it was designed to be the ultimate weapon.

Zap! Zap! Zap! The darkness of space lit up with the green fire of lasers as the Death Star's cannons took aim at Red Squadron. Luckily, the X-wings were designed to move with speed and agility.

Back on the rebel base, Princess Leia and C-3PO anxiously watched the battle on a digital screen.

"This is Red Five. I'm going in," Luke said. He dove toward the surface, firing at the cannons. The Death Star's cannons responded with a storm of laser blasts.

"Luke, pull up!" Biggs warned him.

Luke's blasts had damaged the surface of the Death Star, creating a huge burst of fire.

Luke had no choice but to fly through the flames. Biggs held his breath until Luke emerged from the destruction—unhurt.

"I got a little cooked, but I'm okay," Luke reported.

Another message came in from the rebel command center: "Enemy fighters coming your way!"

Luke checked his visual scanner. Six compact TIE fighters were speeding toward the rebels.

A TIE fighter fired at one of the Red Squadron ships.

Boom! The X-wing exploded.

Another TIE fighter targeted Biggs. Luke swooped in to help his old friend. His targeting system locked on the TIE fighter.

Boom! Luke took it out before it could hit Biggs.

Just then, Gold Squadron started its attack run. The Y-wing fighters streaked through space toward the Death Star. Red Squadron tried to keep the TIE fighters busy. But more TIE fighters were on the way—and Darth Vader himself was piloting one of them!

Three Y-wing fighters entered the trench on the Death Star. They locked their targeting computers on the port.

Then the Death Star's cannons stopped shooting. That could mean only one thing: the TIE fighters had entered the trench, too!

"I'll take them myself," Darth Vader said. "Cover me!"

Green laser blasts fired from Vader's TIE fighter. The expert pilot took down three Y-wings, one after another. Gold Squadron had failed.

Only six members of Red Squadron remained. Red Leader flew into the trench with Red Ten and Red Twelve. Luke, Wedge, and Biggs hung back to cover their friends.

Zoom! Commander Dreis, Red Leader, led the charge through the trench. His targeting system locked on the port. But then, out of nowhere, three TIE fighters swooped down. The trench lit up as they blasted Red Ten and Red Twelve out of existence.

Dreis clenched his teeth and aimed for the target. He released his torpedoes. . . . *Boom!* They hit the Death Star. But they had missed the target.

"I just lost my starboard engine!" Dreis yelled over the comms. "Get set up for your attack run!"

It was all up to Luke, Wedge, and Biggs now.

As their three X-wings entered the trench, a TIE fighter zapped Wedge's ship.

"Get clear!" Luke warned, and Wedge steered out of the trench.

Inside his TIE fighter, Darth Vader kept his focus on Luke.

"The Force is strong with this one," Vader said as Luke expertly dodged his attacks.

"Artoo, try and increase the power!" Luke told his droid.

Behind the remaining two X-wings, the three enemy fighters got closer and closer. Vader took aim at Biggs.

The sky filled with orange flames as Biggs's fighter exploded.

Now Luke was the only pilot who could destroy the Death Star.

Luke was almost in range. He was looking through the targeting scope when he heard Obi-Wan's voice again. *Use the Force, Luke.*

Luke hesitated. Could he do it without the scope? He hadn't needed one to take down the womp rats back home.

He remembered his Jedi lessons with Obi-Wan on the *Millennium Falcon.* Even with a blast shield covering his eyes, he had been able to deflect laser blasts from a floating droid.

Luke turned off his targeting system.

Down in the trench, Darth Vader locked on to Luke's X-wing fighter.

But before Vader could fire . . . *bam!* A blast rocked his ship.

The *Millennium Falcon* swooped down, attacking Vader and the TIE

fighters. Han and Chewbacca had come back to help Luke!

"Yahoo!" Han cheered as he took out two of the ships. His next blast

sent Darth Vader spiraling away into space.

Luke gripped the thrusters of the X-wing. This was it—the Rebel

Alliance's last chance.

The Force flowed through Luke. He could feel it now. Even without his targeting system, he knew just the right moment to fire his torpedoes. Then he flew away from the Death Star as fast as he could.

BOOM! The Death Star exploded into millions of pieces.

A short while later, Princess Leia presented Luke and Han with medals of honor. It was a proud day for the Rebellion. For the first time, it had won a major victory against the Galactic Empire. There was hope for the future.

A new chapter was about to begin.